UNDERCOVER
MISSION SPIES

UNDERCOVER MISSION SPIES

PRISCILLA WAY YUN

PARTRIDGE
A Penguin Random House Company

Library of Congress Control Number: 2015943632
ISBN: Softcover   978-1-4828-3194-8
               eBook   978-1-4828-3195-5

To order additional copies of this book, contact
Toll Free 800 101 2657 (Singapore)
Toll Free 1 800 81 7340 (Malaysia)
orders.singapore@partridgepublishing.com

www.partridgepublishing.com/singapore

CONTENTS

Contents

ACKNOWLEDGEMENT

Without the help of several people, this book would not even exist. First of all, I would like to give thanks to my parents; Michelle and Jimmy Yun for making all of these possible, for helping me find the right resources and facilitating the book publication. I would also like to thank Elaine Seah for assisting me with the grammatical improvements. Besides, I extend my gratitude to those who have lent a hand in reviewing the book and providing me comments for further improvements to my book such as Karis Ng, Samantha Yun and Edwina Horler. Lastly, I would like to thank my brother, Josh Dean Yun for giving me inspiration and support.

CHAPTER 1

MOVING ON

"Destiny! Dean! Let's go! If we don't leave now, you're going to be late!" Mom shouted. Dean and I headed down the stairs with our school bags on and shouted back, "We're coming, we're coming!"

Dean and I are twins of age 13, except that he's a boy and I'm a girl, well you get the rest... Dad got a new job in a little town called Dashtille, and you know when one parent has got to leave, the REST of the family has to follow. Dean and I are heading to school for our last day, to pack the rest of our things in school.

"Mom, can you tell us AGAIN why we have to move?" Dean groaned. Mom patiently said, "For the hundredth time Dean, if you want to survive on money, we've got to go! The new company your Dad's working for is paying for the new house and bills in Dashtille. This is a once in a lifetime opportunity Dean, and we can't miss this out." "But why must things change? Isn't everything good enough right now?" Dean droned on. "Yea, Mom, for the first time, I'm actually agreeing with Dean. I'm in the seventh grade

1

now, and I'm starting to get more popular. Why is it that every time something good happens to me, someone is there to ruin it? This is so unfair!" I continued. "Look kids, you might not know that maybe change is good. Okay? So get in the car because I do not want to talk to the principal about how many times you two have been late, NOT on your last day of school."

When we arrived at school, the school specially organised a farewell ceremony for Dean and me. There was a huge banner plastered across the hall that read "Farewell Destiny and Dean" and then speeches were spoken, songs were sung, and gifts were given. After the farewell, Dean and I went to our classroom lockers and started clearing out our things. "Destiny! Must you leave?" "Yea, must you leave?" Chelsea and Jade lamented. "I'm sorry you guys, but my Dad got a new job... But we can still call each other," I responded. After clearing up our things, Dean and I headed to the round a bout to wait for our parents. Jade, Chelsea and I gave goodbye hugs and bid farewell to one another while Dean stood at a corner staring at us weirdly. He said, "Seriously?" Then I replied calmly, "at least I have friends." He just looked away and muttered to himself.

Soon, our parents arrived. Dean and I went into the car. When I stepped into the car, a man wearing a hooded black coat approached me. He passed me a package and before I could see his face, he left. I was still stunned when Dean pulled me into the car. I shut the door and my Dad drove us out of the school. I waved at Jade and Chelsea goodbye, while they stood at the round a bout in tears, and I looked away before I started crying too. Then Dean asked, "Who was that? And what did he give you?" I was still in shock at that moment and stammered, "I have no idea… I didn't even catch a glimpse of his face…"

Still holding the box and staring at it, Dean nudged me and said, "Well? Are you gonna open the package or not?" I looked at him then looked back at the package and opened it. In it, was a scroll and a small elegant-looking box. I took out the scroll and read it while Dean peered over my shoulder. On it was written:

> Dear Destiny,
>
> After moving to Dashtille, your entire life will change. You may not know who I am but I know who you are. Don't be afraid…
>
> You will meet new people, new places, and new adventures….
>
> Destiny, you and your brother are destined to be in Dashtille, but just remember to trust the right people and be careful…
>
> Open the gifts I have given you two…
>
> I trust that you'll be brave and strong - this is your destiny…
>
> Yours truly,
> Coronel Lestaphirl (I will meet you soon)

After Dean and I read the scroll, we looked at each other with anticipation as we lived for adventures and wondered to ourselves if this was our big break. We were mixed with emotions, both excited and scared. Then, I took the elegant-looking box and opened it. Inside were a silver key necklace with a heart-shaped hole in the middle and a dog tag necklace with a shuriken chained to it.

There was also a tiny note in it. It said: "The key is to be worn by Destiny and the dog tag is to be worn by Dean. They should be worn at all times, even when showering. These are meant to protect you from evil, so be alert, as they are everywhere. They can also come in handy during your missions, but you'll have to find me first as part of your training. Good luck! I know you can do it but you'll have to make a few friends first…. Again, Coronel Lestaphirl" Dean took the dog tag and wore it while I took the key necklace and put it on too.

Chapter 2

FRIENDS

When we arrived, we checked out our new rooms, Dean and I shared a bedroom together and my parents shared a master bedroom down the hall. After we un-packed our luggages in our brand new rooms, my parents suggested Dean and I to walk around the neighbourhood to make new friends. Dean and I stepped out of the house and went to the field right in front of our house and sat at the swings. The houses in the neighbourhood were built in a circle, surrounding a field with a big elm tree in the middle and two swings hanging on two thick branches of the elm tree. In my eyes, the neighbourhood seemed really calm and relaxing.

A few minutes later, two boys and a girl, all the same age as Dean and me, headed towards us. One of the boys said, "Hey! You must be the new kids who just moved in, right?" Dean and I replied together, "Yep!" Then, I stood up from the swing and reached out my hand and said, "Hi! I'm Destiny and this is my twin brother, Dean." Dean also stood up, reached out his hand and all of us took turns shaking

5

hands and exchanging names. The girl's name was Cassidy, her brother's name was Jake and the other boy was Dylan, who had been friends with them for years.

Cassidy had long surf-like hair loose and wavy, flowing down her back, she was wearing a plain white T-shirt with the words "dance" written on it and a pair of jean shorts. Jake had short hair that covered part of his eye; he wore a jersey shirt with Bermuda shorts. Dylan's hair was parted right down the middle, which flowed down to his ear, he wore a pair of black round spectacles; he wore a long-sleeved shirt with a sweater vest above it and long pants.

"So, how long have you all been living here?" I asked. "Ummm… about five years, right guys?" Cassidy asked Jake and Dylan and both the boys nodded their heads. "Well, ummm… Do you know a guy named Coronel Lestaphirl?" Dean blurted out. I stared at Dean with the what-do-you-think-you're-doing look. Dean just ignored me. Cassidy, Jake and Dylan looked at each other knowingly and Jake finally said, "Oh, so YOU guys are them…" Dean and I looked at each other questioningly.

"Coronel Lestaphirl is the head of the UMS…" Dylan started but was interrupted by Cassidy, who said, "UMS stands for Undercover Mission Spies. We go through different stages of mysterious missions to finally complete all our missions to graduate and fight real crimes. Because the evil villains are everywhere, and we have to get rid of them, we have missions…" "And as I was saying," Jake jumped in, "Mr Coronel told us to show you the UMS door in your house. So, can we go in?" "Ummm… sure!" I said and we headed towards our house.

When we stepped into the house, Mom approached us and welcomed Cassidy, Jake and Dylan with warm greetings and said to Dean and me, "Wow, you guys have made new friends really fast!" "Yea... but they..." I started to respond but Jake pushed me towards our room, which had our names pasted on the door and said, "Thank you! We better get going to know more about each other, okay, bye!" Instantly, all of us ended up in our room. "What was that for?" I asked Jake. "Sorry, it just seems like you were about to tell your mom about the UMS which you're not supposed to..." Jake answered. I just replied apologetically, "Oh... sorry."

In the room, the bunk beds that Dean and I shared were placed at the corner and a circular carpet in the middle; and light switches were at the side of the door. Two desks were placed at the other corner of the room, opposite the bunk beds, facing the wall and two large black and white sack bags sat beside the bunk beds. Finally, two huge closets placed at the other corner of the room.

Once everybody got into the room, Jake shut and locked the door behind him. "Okay, now the door will be revealed..." Cassidy said mystically. "Would you like to do the honours, Dylan?" Cassidy turned to Dylan and then she continued, "Because he always loves to open the entrances..." "Yep, it's true." Jake faced Dylan.

Dylan headed towards the light switch and opened the light switch panel. Dean and I were puzzled but also headed to the light switch panel after being told to do so. Apparently, under the light switch panel was a thumbprint scanner!

Dylan explained to us that all of the UMS members' rooms have a thumbprint scanner, which can only be used by the UMS members. Then, Dylan instructed either Dean or me to scan our thumbprint. Dean and I started arguing whose thumb should be scanned and started pushing and nudging each other. Finally, Jake said, "Oh for goodness sake, just flip a coin! Destiny's heads, and Dean's tails." Dean and I agreed and Jake tossed the coin in the air and caught it, then he said, "And…. It's tails! Dean, scan your thumb on the thumbprint scanner." Dean stuck out his tongue at me and scanned his thumbprint.

Immediately, the carpet opened, Dean and I stared blankly and gaped in shock as our jaws dropped. All five of us looked down and saw colourful fluffy pillows and sack bags. Our shocked mouths turned into a huge wide smile and exclaimed, "Awesome!" At Cassidy's suggestion, all of us held hands surrounding the hole, and then at the count of 3 from her, all of us would jump in.

CHAPTER 3

THE LAB

WhEN Cassidy, Jake, Dylan, Dean and I jumped in, we landed in a pool of fluffy, soft pillows and multi-coloured sack bags. "Cool!" Dean and I shouted in unison. "Where are we?" I asked Cassidy. "We are in an enclosed elevator but Mr Coronel designed it to be played in and for conveniences like a library, a changing room with unlimited clothes of your sizes and a food court to eat in if you're hungry. The rest of the stuff is to relax and have fun as the journey to the lab takes some time so in the mean time we can play! Oh! There's also a button to change the design you want to have in the elevator. Mr Coronel always invent new modes in the elevator so we can test it out too!"

We could feel the elevator moving downwards but we were too distracted to notice it. Cassidy headed to a panel, the only panel in the elevator, which states 'CHANGE' and under it has a few buttons and labels beside them.

Suddenly, Cassidy and I reached out our hands and pressed the button with 'Trampoline' beside it together at the same time. Then both of us shouted, "JINX! DOUBLE-JINX! TRIPLE-JINX! QUADRIPLE-JINX! INFINTY-JINX!" together and finally I shouted "YOU OWE ME A SODA!" first, so Cassidy owed me a soda.

Suddenly, the fluffy, soft pillows and multi-coloured sack bags disappeared and all of us ended up sitting on a huge trampoline that covered the entire elevator. All of us started jumping up and down on the trampoline, screaming and laughing happily. This was how all five of us bonded even more strongly. We had so much fun jumping around, doing somersaults and knowing more about each other.

Soon, the elevator stopped, jerked a little and the elevator door slid open. I did a front flip out of the elevator and the rest all cheered. Dean did a 360 spin, Cassidy did a cartwheel, Jake did a double flip but Dylan just walked out of the trampoline. All of us stared at Dylan with an eyebrow raised and Dylan just answered calmly, "What? I like to be mainstream." "Dylan isn't really the one who does the tricks and somersaults, he's the one with the brains and smarts, am I right Dylan?" a gentle voice remarked. All of us turned around and saw a man in his thirties in a well-dressed business suit, neat-combed dark black hair with smart-looking spectacles. "Let me introduce myself," he moved towards Dean and me and welcomed us. "Hello, I am Mr Coronel Lestaphirl," he said and shook our hands.

Immediately, Dean and I started asking many questions like: How do you know us? What are the necklaces for? What is going to happen to us? Why do you want us? Are we in trouble? Mr Coronel just replied, "Whoa, whoa, whoa!

Slow down! Don't worry. I'll answer all your questions after I have shown you the lab and everybody's strategies."

Mr Coronel showed us the pure white lab with several computers, electronic gadgets and physical training equipment like treadmills, stationary bicycles and more. There were also rooms for visual training, reaction training, etc.

After showing Dean and me around the lab with Cassidy, Jake and Dylan tagging behind, Mr Coronel continued by explaining why he had specifically chosen the five of us for the UMS, telling us our abilities and our use for the UMS. Following that, Mr Coronel declared to us that Dean and I were the last recruits as both of us had the talents and abilities that could compliment the three to complete missions. Though Dean and I were confused, we just nodded our heads and went along with the group.

After a long and very detailed lecture, he explained to us why we were chosen…

Undercover Mission Spies
New Recruits

Name: Destiny Andrews
Ability: Gymnastic
Strategy: Flexible, Knows Somersaults and Stunts

Name: Dean Andrews
Ability: Karate (Black Belt)
Strategy: Good at Defending and Strong Physically

Name: Cassidy Lansford
Ability: Hip Hop Dancer
Strategy: Knows how to move Smoothly, Flexible and Somersaults

Name: Jake Lansford
Ability: Athlete
Strategy: Good at Sports, Fast moving and Multi-tasking

Name: Dylan Lestaphirl (Mr Coronel's son)
Ability: Smart
Strategy: Fast problem solver and Good Memory

CHAPTER 4

EXPLORATION

After the explanation and the tour around the lab, Mr Coronel brought us into a screening room. Then, he said, "Now, I'm going to answer your questions by showing you all a video clip…" He turned around and as the screen moved downwards, he pressed some buttons on a remote control. It was a video of me, when I was four years old, doing my gymnastics routine on a balance beam. Mr Coronel said, "I chose you," and faced me, "Destiny, because of your talent in gymnastics at a very young age. You are absolutely flexible and you know good stunts to avoid things being hurled by simply flipping away; and that's what I need in the UMS."

Mr Coronel switched the video to Dean in a karate match slamming his opponent down. Mr Coronel continued, "Dean is a black belt in karate, so you are good in attacking and defending when being provoked. Hence, if anybody tries to hurt you during your missions, you can fight and attack the bad guys with help by the others, of course."

Then, Mr Coronel pressed another button on the remote control and the video switched to Cassidy dancing hip-hop, break-dancing and other tricky and swift moves. Mr Coronel continued to say, "Cassidy has a gift in dancing, of all types. You have been dancing since three years old. You have the ability to duck, kick, double-flip, jump and move swiftly with grace and style."

After that, the video was switched again, but now to Jake, who was multi-tasking, spinning a basketball on one finger while kicking a soccer ball doing tricks. "Jake is very good at sports and is fast-moving. When something is hurled at you, your reaction time is faster than an average person, so you will be able to defend yourself by blocking the object in one swift move, hence an advantage to the team." Mr Coronel praised Jake.

Mr Coronel then changed the video to Dylan pointing at a pie chart of gases of oxygen, nitrogen, etc. while blabbering about the contents of the gases. Mr Coronel continued, "And last but not least, Dylan. Since you were just two years old, you have already learnt how to read your first Encyclopedia. With your smarts, during your missions, you can help the team solve situational problems in no time. As long as all of you put your skills and talents together, you can solve any situational mission in no time."

After Mr Coronel has finished with the video clips, Dean blurted out, "So, you have been stalking us? And how did you know us since we were young?" All of us started laughing. Mr Coronel chuckled and answered, "Of course not, but I'm not allowed to tell you... I'm sorry, it is confidential."

After getting to know the UMS better, Mr Coronel gave us a mini-mission to get through together. Mr Coronel said that the mission was to get all of us to work together as a team and to figure out how to use our abilities to solve the mystery together.

Mr Coronel specially built a virtual portal for all of us to enter as part of our first mission together. We were to complete all the stages in the virtual portal to accomplish this mission. After wishing us luck, Mr Coronel pushed all of us into a room and locked the door. Then, all of us heard a voice, "I can see and hear everything that you are doing, so don't be afraid, this is just a test-run, totally unreal. Your first task is to exit the room, which will lead all of you to a passage; and by putting all your heads together; you all will have no problem completing the mission. The passage has different stages for all of you to figure out your hidden abilities and is also part of your training. Good luck and let your quest began!"

The room was dim and empty, except with a few boxes at the corner of the room. Dean and Jake decided to check out the boxes, hoping to find something useful while the rest of the team figure out how to open the door. Cassidy and I headed to observe the door, while Dylan visualized the room by trying to "scan it into his brain".

Suddenly, Jake shouted out, "Hey guys! We found something!" Cassidy, Dylan and I went to Jake and Dean's side to see what they had found. Dean held out a piece of pink heart-shaped diamond jewel in one hand and a blue, a yellow, a green and a transparent crystal in the other.

"Hey! The heart-shaped jewel looks like the same shape as the heart-shaped hole in the key necklace that you're wearing, Destiny," Cassidy exclaimed with delight and handed the pink heart-shaped diamond jewel to me. I took it and held out my key necklace that hung on my neck. I placed the pink jewel in the heart-shaped hole in my necklace and it fitted perfectly! We were all amazed by that but not as amazed as when my pink heart-shaped diamond jewel started glowing and the key started 'floating' in the air.

I was standing directly in front of Dean, whose hand still held out the blue, yellow, green and transparent crystals. The key was glowing very brightly, 'floating' and pointing towards the green crystal.

After detailed observation, Dylan said that the hole on the door has the same size and shape as the green crystal. Cassidy then took the green crystal and placed it in the hole on the door. I stood in front of the door as the key on my necklace shined brightly and moved closer to the green crystal now in the hole on the door.

At that very moment, there was a blinding flash and the door opened! All five of us started cheering our success and Mr Coronel congratulated us, "Well done, kids! You have succeeded the first part of the test. Now you have to complete the following stages, which I will lead you through. So, good luck once again!"

CHAPTER 5

CHANGING

We went through the door and ended up in another room. There were two changing rooms at the corner of the room and piles of clothes, accessories and shoes scattered everywhere. At the end of the room, there were alarm gates in front of an exit. Then, Mr Coronel's voice was projected again, "At this stage, you first have to find the riddle and figure out how to solve it before continuing on to the next stage. If you pass the alarm gates successfully, the exit will be unlocked."

Jake tried to walk pass the alarm gates but a loud siren triggered and the exit was locked. "I think this is the riddle…" Cassidy said as she bent down and sat on the floor. All of us went to her side to see what she was looking at. We saw some writing on the floor but it seemed all scribbled and in gibberish. Dylan bent down and examined the writing and finally said, "It's in Spanish." All of us looked at him and said altogether, "Huh?" "The writing is in Spanish!" Dylan continued and all of us said with a questioning tone, "You speak Spanish?" "Just a little," Dylan said, "my mother is a Spaniard and used to teach me a little bit of Spanish before she… she… she… passed away…" All of us felt sad for him but didn't know how to comfort him so there was an awkward silence until Dean broke the silence and said, "So, can you translate it for us, Dylan?"

Dylan then said, "Sure! The writing says, 'Through life, people need to change for the better, but what happens when trouble comes, for five who need to change, to be based on what they are'."

"I think what it means is that we need to change something of ourselves," Dean suggested. "CLOTHES!" I exclaimed, "Look around! There are piles of clothes everywhere! I think we're supposed to change our outfits to fit who we are. For instance, Dean is a black belt in karate, so he should wear a karate gi and a black belt. Since Cassidy is a hip-hop dancer, she should wear a hip-hop outfit like a singlet, baggy pants and a snapback. Jake should wear a jersey, track uniform and spike shoes. Dylan should wear a white coat and protective eye-wear; and I can wear a gymnastic uniform like the leotard." "That's great! Let's do it!" Cassidy shouted.

All of us rummaged through the piles of clothes, accessories and shoes to change in with my help to show them how to match clothes and accessories together. After that, all of us changed into our own individual outfits in the changing room and we looked totally awesome! All of us walked pass the alarm gates successfully and pass through the exit.

Mr Coronel's voice was then projected again, "Great! You all have passed this stage! This stage was for Destiny to discover the fact that she has talent in fashion and disguising features. During a mission, Destiny can help with the disguises to blend in with the crowd and not to look too suspicious. So, congratulations! You may all proceed to the next level!"

CHAPTER 6

TIME TO DANCE

On the next level, we found ourselves in a corridor with multi-coloured blinking tiles. Mr Coronel then instructed, "Now, you're in the dance level. You have to dance your way through the corridor, in a correct pattern to avoid getting hit with consequences. Good luck!"

After a few seconds, I shouted out, "I've got it!" Cassidy, Jake, Dylan and Dean all looked at me with anticipation. Then, I continued, "All the stages here are to train and test our abilities, then who's the one here who's got the moves like Jagger? Of course, that would be Cassidy! So, she can dance her way across the tiles to the end!" "That's great, except there're two problems. How would Cassidy know exactly which dance and tiles to step on? And, how are we supposed to follow her moves?" Jake pointed out and I simply muttered, "How do I know? I just solved part of the problem..." After several minutes of thorough examination of the room, Dylan spoke out, "Beside the door at the end of the room, there is a 'STOP' button which I think is to

21

switch off the booby traps. But on what type of dance, I don't know." "Okay, we got that part solved. Maybe there's a clue in here somewhere to find out what type of dance and I don't think the booby traps would be THAT bad…" Dean responded lightly while stepping onto the first tile in front him. Out of nowhere, a dart flew out and was almost going to hit Dean. Fortunately, he realised it coming his way and with one swift move, he dodged the dart, which ended up hitting the wall. Dean then said sheepishly, "Forget what I said, and just find that clue before our heads get cut off."

We searched around the room for any sort of clue or note, like the one we found in the room before, but there was nothing. Soon, Cassidy exclaimed, "Hey! I found a knob but it is missing a handle to turn the knob." "The crystal!" Dean exclaimed with a tinge of excitement and took out the remaining blue, yellow and transparent crystals in his pocket. Dylan stepped forward, observed carefully and finally said that the yellow crystal was the exact shape and size of the knob holder for the handle and the yellow crystal was the only one that was long enough to use as a handle.

Dean handed Cassidy the yellow crystal and she placed it and locked in the knob handle holder. It fitted perfectly! Cassidy turned the knob a few times and music prevailed over the air. Then Cassidy exclaimed, "I know this song! It's one of the hip-hop songs I learned and it has specific routines. I haven't done them for a long time and I may not remember but it doesn't hurt to try…"

Cassidy did a double flip onto a blue blinking tile then she started dancing smoothly and in style. She clapped her hands, did the dougie, slipped and slide, handstands, headstands and many other cool hip hop dance moves. We clapped and cheered her on and were in awe. After her last move, Jake then mocked her by saying, "And you said you didn't remember?"

Cassidy flipped her hair back, pressed the 'STOP' button and turned back to us. We were uncertain if the booby traps were totally switched off, so I pushed Dean, who was standing right in front of me, towards the tiles. He jerked a bit and no booby traps appeared. So, Jake, Dylan, Dean and I walked briskly and calmly across the corridor of tiles.

CHAPTER 7

REACTIONS

O n the next level, we found ourselves in a corridor with multi-coloured blinking tiles. Mr Coronel then instructed, "Now, you're in the dance level. You have to dance your way through the corridor, in a correct pattern to avoid getting hit with consequences. Good luck!"

After a few seconds, I shouted out, "I've got it!" Cassidy, Jake, Dylan and Dean all looked at me with anticipation. Then, I continued, "All the stages here are to train and test our abilities, then who's the one here who's got the moves like Jagger? Of course, that would be Cassidy! So, she can dance her way across the tiles to the end!" "That's great, except there're two problems. How would Cassidy know exactly which dance and tiles to step on? And, how are we supposed to follow her moves?" Jake pointed out and I simply muttered, "How do I know? I just solved part of the problem…" After several minutes of thorough examination of the room, Dylan spoke out, "Beside the door at the end of the room, there is a 'STOP' button which I think is to switch off the booby traps. But on what type of dance, I don't know." "Okay, we got that part solved. Maybe there's a clue in here somewhere to find out what type of dance and I don't think the booby traps would be THAT bad…" Dean responded lightly while stepping onto the first tile in front him. Out of nowhere, a dart flew out and was almost going to hit Dean. Fortunately, he realised it coming his way and with one swift move, he dodged the dart, which ended up hitting the wall. Dean then said sheepishly, "Forget what I said, and just find that clue before our heads get cut off."

We searched around the room for any sort of clue or note, like the one we found in the room before, but there was nothing. Soon, Cassidy exclaimed, "Hey! I found a knob but it is missing a handle to turn the knob." "The crystal!" Dean exclaimed with a tinge of excitement and took out the remaining blue, yellow and transparent crystals in his pocket. Dylan stepped forward, observed carefully and finally said that the yellow crystal was the exact shape and size of the knob holder for the handle and the yellow crystal was the only one that was long enough to use as a handle.

Dean handed Cassidy the yellow crystal and she placed it and locked in the knob handle holder. It fitted perfectly! Cassidy turned the knob a few times and music prevailed over the air. Then Cassidy exclaimed, "I know this song! It's one of the hip-hop songs I learned and it has specific routines. I haven't done them for a long time and I may not remember but it doesn't hurt to try…"

Cassidy did a double flip onto a blue blinking tile then she started dancing smoothly and in style. She clapped her hands, did the dougie, slipped and slide, handstands, headstands and many other cool hip hop dance moves. We clapped and cheered her on and were in awe. After her last move, Jake then mocked her by saying, "And you said you didn't remember?"

Cassidy flipped her hair back, pressed the 'STOP' button and turned back to us. We were uncertain if the booby traps were totally switched off, so I pushed Dean, who was standing right in front of me, towards the tiles. He jerked a bit and no booby traps appeared. So, Jake, Dylan, Dean and I walked briskly and calmly across the corridor of tiles.

CHAPTER 8

THE ESCAPE

Cassidy, Jake, Dylan and Dean ran across the room to my side and Mr Coronel congratulated us as saying, "You have uncovered Dean and Jake's physical ability to react fast in dangerous times. Now, the last stage to complete your test is to figure out how to escape the room. Once again, good luck!"

As Dean and Jake took time to catch their breaths, Cassidy, Dylan and I started our investigation. Then, Cassidy and I spotted a corner of a note at a meter higher than the keypad and I asked Cassidy to give me a boost. She held her hands out and I stepped on them as she lifted me into the air, allowing me to grab the piece of note nicely and landing safely to the ground. I held the note in front of me then said, "Dylan? Would you please translate this? It's obviously not a language we know…" "Gladly," Dylan replied with no hesitation or whatsoever. He read aloud, "Invisibility is the key. Once you find it, you'll be free."

All of us started thinking and mumbling to ourselves. "I've got it!" Jake shouted, "'Invisibility is the key' probably means that the door is invisible and we have to find it. Once we find it, we'll be free!" "Great! Now, how do we find the invisible door?" Dean questioned. All of us, once again, went back into thinking. Dylan finally broke the silence and said, "Since the door is invisible, we have to find something to make it 'UN-invisible'! And to do that, we need something to spray it; either powder or water, and we can spray the substance around the room until we see something appearing." "But does anyone here have that?" Cassidy asked. All of us looked around as I pulled something out of my pocket. "I have a perfume... but... it's brand new..." I stammered then sighed, "but to get out of the room... just take it!" I said dramatically, held out the perfume and looked away. Cassidy took the perfume from my hand and assured me, "It's okay, we're not gonna waste it. I promise. Just a few sprits won't hurt, right?" After thinking for a while, I nodded my head.

Cassidy sprayed the walls of the room a few times and suddenly, the room started quaking and shaking and one side of the wall, slid open. All of us stepped out together and saw Mr Coronel smiling at us. He started cheering and heaping praises on us saying, "I knew you kids could do it! The last test was for Dylan to train his smarts and translation ability, which would be good for future missions. Congratulations to all of you! You have all succeeded working together and uncovering your hidden abilities!"

Mr Coronel handed each of us a hearing device and explained, "Put this hearing device in your ear at all times; this will help all of you to keep in contact with each other. This is my latest invention; nothing can destroy it or hurt you. Even when you shower, you will not be electrocuted. Does that answer your question, Jake?" He turned towards Jake whose hand was in the air but slowly descended back down and all of us started laughing.

CHAPTER 9

COMMUNICATION

"Dean! Destiny and friends! Time for dinner!" a voice shouted. Mr Coronel had turned on one of the small television screens on his desk, which showed camera footage of Mom calling for us outside our room for dinner with a lady standing beside her. "The UMS has set up cameras at the big elm tree that faces each of your houses and inside your houses to let us know when you have to go back home or if there is any danger coming your way. And apparently, it's time for all of you to go home as Mrs. Andrews has met Mrs. Lansford," Mr Coronel said while gesturing us to the elevator, "I'll continue to speak to all of you in the elevator."

As we got into the elevator, Mr Coronel's face appeared on the elevator wall; apparently we were Skyping. He said, "While you all were taking the test, Mrs. Andrews met Mrs. Lansford. Apparently Mrs. Lansford has invited all of you to have dinner together! And Dylan, you may eat with them, but if they ask for me, tell them that I have many things on my hands right now; maybe another time to meet up would be nice. Have fun at dinner! I'll be watching over all of you! And by the way, you may press the button beside the "CHANGE" panel that would boost the speed of the elevator to get to your room." In the twinkling of an eye, Mr Coronel's face disappeared from the elevator wall. I pressed the speed button and soon we were back into our room.

I opened the door and Mom introduced Mrs. Lansford to Dean and me while Mrs. Lansford introduced Cassidy, Jake and Dylan to Mom. After warm greetings and exchanging of questions, all of us headed to Cassidy and Jake's home for dinner.

The Lansford's home was very elegant. Mrs. Lansford brought us to the dining room where a long, wooden, grand table surrounded by 16 chairs stood; above it was a bright crystal chandelier. All of us took a seat, chatting, smiling and laughing around the table. Soon, the table was laid with scrumptious and mouth-watering food, and we all had a whale of a time. After dinner, Cassidy, Jake, Dylan, Dean and I exchanged phone numbers and created a group for all five of us to communicate together more efficiently.

That night, I turned from side to side trying to find a comfortable position but I just could not sleep. I turned so much that I fell off my bed, which was the top bunk, and landed fortunately on the soft and cushiony carpet with a thud which evidently woke Dean up who wasn't really sleeping either. "Can't sleep huh?" Dean asked me who was still kind of groaning on the floor. "Yea… You too?" I replied. "Yea… I mean there are so many things in my mind right now and everything is so confusing…" Dean replied clutching his head. "Hey!" I suggested, "Why don't we message the group and see if they're sleeping? If we can't sleep, we might as well do something to pass time!" "I guess…" Dean said as he started rummaging his things to find his phone while I climbed up to my bed to take my phone.

Then, Dean and I sat comfortably on the carpet, whipped out our mobile phones and started texting the group and hoping for a response from them.

UMS (chat group)

Destiny :   Hello? Anyone online? Can't sleep…

Dean :   Yea…

Cassidy :   Hey… Can't sleep too… Don't know why…

Destiny :   Yay! At least you're awake too…

Dean :   Yea… Hey! Is Jake awake?

Jake :   Wassup!

Destiny :   Yay! Everyone's here except for Dylan…

Dylan :   Now what makes you think I'm not here?

Cassidy :   Hey Dylan!

Destiny :   Hi Dylan!

Jake :   Wassup! :D

Dean :   Why aren't you guys sleeping? 'Cause I thought for sure u were…

Destiny :   Same reason you aren't? Can't sleep! Duh?

Cassidy :   Well… Let's change the subject b4 the Andrews twins over here get into a heated argument…

Jake :	Oh ya! Dean and Destiny, which school would you be enrolling in tomorrow?
Destiny :	Ummm... Lemme see... We're going to Middleton High School
Jake :	That's great! We're in that school too! Then we can tour u around and help u guys out! We'll be closer this way...
Destiny :	Great!
Jake :	Why don't we all meet up together in the morning after breakfast under the big elm tree at 8am? Then we can all walk to school together!
Destiny :	Sure! Why not?
Dean :	See you there!
Cassidy :	Ok
Dylan :	Sure! Gd nite!
Jake :	Nites!

After the mini-chat, all of us went back to sleep and slept peacefully the whole night.

Chapter 10

SCHOOL

The next morning, my alarm went off and as I reached out my hand to press the snooze button, I heard Mom yelling us to wake up. I leapt up from my bed, woke Dean up by shaking him vigorously and then headed to the bathroom. After washing up and changing, I opened the bathroom door to find Dean leaning against the wall, half-asleep. I had a sly smile on my face then at the top of my voice, I screamed, "DEAN!!!! WAKE UP!!!" Dean shot up into the air with alarm and thanked me groggily for waking him up, then proceeded into the bathroom. I carried my bag and walked down the stairs for breakfast. Soon, Dean came down too.

After breakfast, I looked at my watch and suggested, "Hey Dean! It's 7:50am, let's go sit on the swings and wait for Cassidy, Jake and Dylan." "Ok," Dean agreed. We carried our bags and headed for the swings. Soon, Cassidy, Jake and Dylan arrived and we set off to school.

Upon arriving, we bumped into the principal, Mrs. Jacque. Cassidy, Jake and Dylan introduced us to the principal and said that Dean and I were new comers. The three then volunteered to tour both of us around the school, which Mrs. Jacque kindly agreed to. Mrs. Jacque shook our hands, greeted us courteously and gave us our class schedule then left the three to tour us around the school until assembly. Cassidy explained to me the class schedule and that every subject was in a different classroom. Fortunately all 5 of us were in the same grade and group, so we had the exact same class schedule, and they could guide us to each classroom.

Then, Cassidy, Jake and Dylan gave us a tour around the school. Dean and I kept "oooh-ing" and "aaah-ing" whenever we saw something fascinating and cool. We soon realised that Ridgeway High had more advanced and high-tech facilities than in our previous school. Both of us were attached to the new school and had soon forgotten the heartache about leaving our old home.

"Ring…" the school bell rang and prevailed over the background noise of the pupil's chattering; everybody headed towards the hall orderly for assembly. We stepped into this huge hall, which looked more like a cinema theatre, with rows and rows of cinema chairs progressing all the way down. Dean and I gasped as we walked down the steps. Cassidy, Jake and Dylan led us to the front row where we sat down and took in the smell of a new beginning.

During the assembly, Mrs. Jacque started off with introducing Dean and me, the newbies, to the school. We felt very much welcome by the school through their smiling faces and friendly gestures that indicate "hello", "hey", "welcome on board" and "welcome to the Ridgeway community" etc. The Principle continued on with other activities related announcements before she dismissed the assembly.

While Cassidy, Jake and Dylan led Dean and me to the English class, Cassidy told us that there's nothing to be nervous about; yet, as we inched closer and closer to the classroom, our hearts were palpitating wildly and our hands were clammy, not knowing what would happen.

After we got into the classroom, all of us took a sit. Cassidy and I sat together while Dean and Jake sat behind us respectively. Only poor Dylan with no partner sat at the next table beside Jake and Dean. Soon, a man with a thick moustache walked into the classroom. He said, "Good morning class, we have two new students in our class today, Dean and Destiny." He turned to us and invited us to stand in front of the class and introduce ourselves. "Hello, I'm Mr Jepson, the class English teacher. It's nice to meet you; I hope you will enjoy your first day of school." Dean and I thanked him and went back to our seats.

As we sat down, I caught a glimpse of three Goth girls (with black make-up, black clothing and piercings; they looked more like punk rock rebels to me) staring at me. I leaned towards Cassidy and whispered into her ear, "Hey! Do you know who the three Goth girls are? They keep staring at me; it's a little uncomfortable…" "Oh! They're Angie, Alex and Aida; everybody calls them 'The Goths'. I warn you not to mix with them as they are the class rebels, so be careful," Cassidy warned me. I just nodded and Mr Jepson started the class.

During class, Mr Jepson talked about poetry, which was my best subject and I answered most of his questions correctly. Mr Jepson heaped praises over me and 'The Goths' stared at me with annoyance, but I just ignored it.

After class, Cassidy, Jake, Dylan, Dean and I packed our books and walked out of the class. When we got out of the classroom, Jake pulled me aside and said, "Careful... The Goths didn't seem to like you very much..." "Why?" I asked. "Because you're smart! They despise people who are smarter than them and they can do 'things' to you," Jake replied. "Like what? And anyway if this didn't bother me in my old school, it certainly won't bother me now. I take criticism really well." I replied with no hesitation.

As we walked together, Jake, Dean and Dylan walked side by side, talking to each other and I walked behind Jake while talking to Cassidy who was walking behind Dean. The Goths leaned against the wall facing us. Then, Angie stretched out her leg and before I could stop myself from walking, I tripped over her foot and fell on top of Jake who coincidentally turned around. I landed on top of Jake with my palms on the floor, supporting my body so as not to hit Jake. At that moment, our eyes met; I didn't know why, but my heart was beating fast and I felt a warm tingly feeling. Likewise, he felt the same.

After a few seconds of regaining reality, I noticed Dean's arm stretched out towards me, so I grabbed his hand and he pulled me up. When I got up, Jake had already stood up. I was still blur on what had just happened and so was Jake, but I tried to focus. Cassidy asked me if I was okay and I just calmly replied, "Yes." As I turned my head and gazed at Jake, I saw him gazing back. I quickly turned away as I could feel my cheeks burning and I instantly knew that I was blushing.

CHAPTER 11

THE FLYER

After school dismissal, we carried our slightly heavier school bags, already filled with homework, and headed home. On the way home, Dean spotted something amiss and stopped suddenly, causing Cassidy and Dylan who were walking right behind him to bump into him. He bent down and picked up a piece of small crumpled paper on the sidewalk and said, "What's this?" "Why would you care? This place is always being littered..." Jake asked. "Remember during chemistry, we were talking about the rarest kind of gem, the brightest shining object currently found? It could only be found in the middle of the Pacific Ocean due to its natural environment and perfect condition for its growth." Dean questioned us. "You mean the Glaziem crest? What about it?" I responded with an eyebrow raised. "This looks exactly like it in the slideshow we watched during class," Dean said as he started unfolding and straightening the paper, "I think, as a bright gleam caught my eye."

All of us surrounded Dean to take a look at the crumpled piece of note and on top of the paper was a green embroidered crest gem and wavy golden linings beside it. The paper was a flyer about a newly found item to be displayed at Ridgeway Museum for a free entry. The item that looked more like a bejeweled cane to me, was made out of crystals and jewels, and was claimed to be a duplicator from the 80's. Dylan exclaimed, "You are right, Dean! This IS the Glaziem crest! But, how could that be possible? It is impossible to find it here! Only someone who actually lives in the Pacific Ocean could possibly find it, with slim chance though!" Dylan ended with a sarcastic remark and a snort. "Why don't we go home and ask Mr Coronel about this flyer? Maybe he would know something about it." I suggested. "That's a great idea!" Jake exclaimed, a little overly excited. All of us turned around to look at him and as Jake noticed the awkward moment he quickly hurried forward and said, "What are you standing around for? Let's get moving!" Everyone else started giggling and as I giggled, I blushed a little. Trying to hide that, I quickly wore my hoodie and continued on walking.

When we reached the neighbourhood, all of us decided to go back to our own homes and meet up in the elevator after putting our bags down. Apparently, Mr Coronel informed us through our earpiece during school that he had just designed a secret tunnel to the elevator so those in the UMS would only use an elevator and be accompanied by the others. The secret tunnel would be slides, roller coasters or others. It was a different surprise each day!

When we reached home, we saw Mom still busy unpacking the boxes in the living room. We greeted her and she said that we would talk about our first day of school during dinner. After the small chat we had with Mom, Dean and I hurried into our room and locked the door behind us.

I opened the light switch panel and scanned my thumb on the thumbprint scanner. The carpet opened and Dean and I could see two swirly slides as we looked down the hole. We sat on the start of the slide and pushed ourselves down the slides. Our slides were side by side and we went down round and round, swirls, loops in super-fast speed. We could feel our hair flying in the air and we started screaming and shouting, "This is AWESOME!" "WOOHOO!" "COOL!!!" "Yea!"

Soon, we landed in a huge ball pit. When Dean and I landed, Cassidy, Jake and Dylan were already there, throwing the multi-coloured balls at each other. As we fell into the ball pit, Cassidy, Jake and Dylan started throwing the balls at us, which apparently was their way of welcoming us in humour. We all started throwing balls at each other and had a blast. We were screaming, ducking, laughing, and throwing. We had so much fun that we didn't even know that we had already landed until Mr Coronel opened the elevator door and some of the multi-coloured balls fell out.

As Mr Coronel pressed the 'normal' button on another 'CHANGE' panel outside the elevator, he asked Dean and me how the first day of school was. "It was great! I guess..." Dean replied. "Yea! It was not as bad as I thought," I continued. Then, Dean said, "Ya! Destiny answered lots of questions; I signed up for the karate club; The Goth hates Destiny; I got into karate club; The Goth tripped Destiny; I learnt that the school here sells better food than my old school; Destiny and Jake has a thing going on (and at that point, I stared at him hard but he just ignored it and he just kept babbling on); Benjamin Henderson threw up at the sight of a frog and the slides that you added into the elevator was AWESOME!" Mr Coronel seemed a little confused after hearing so much but after a while he processed everything in order as he finally said, "Well, good job Destiny; nice decision and good for training your skills, Dean; sorry Destiny 'bout The Goth; great job for getting into karate club Dean; are you okay, Destiny? I feel sorry for your old school; Dean, that's not very nice; hope someone cleans up Benjamin's mess and I'm glad you like my installation." We all clapped for Mr Coronel as most of us couldn't get everything but he answered all Dean's remarks exactly in order, and said it just as fast as how Dean had it across.

Dean then continued, "We found this on the way back home and we thought it was suspicious so we wondered if you could examine it. It's a flyer to Ridgeway Museum about some duplicator thingy and there's a Glaziem crest on the top of the flyer. We learned that it was very rare and could only be found in the middle of the Pacific Ocean due to its natural environment and perfect condition for its growth. Care to explain?" and passed the crumpled piece of flyer to Mr Coronel. Mr Coronel thanked Dean for the summary of our queries and placed the flyer on his desk. He examined it clearly then gasped with a terrified look and said, "Oh no…"

CHAPTER 12

THE STORY

"O h no? What do you mean by 'oh no'?" I asked anxiously. Then Mr Coronel told us the story...

"In the 80's, I had just started the UMS not for long. My weaponry team had invented that duplicator so as to restore anything that was broken or damaged and to duplicate any item of desire, but someone was after it... and that someone was my old partner, Bane. We were initially a team and wanted to work together to make the duplicator. But, he was jealous of my 'goody goody' work and getting all the praises, so he decided to go against me. Once he learned about the new device that my team had just invented, he was after it, as he wanted to use it for greed. At one time, he ALMOST got away with it. I was in the lab figuring out how to lock the duplicator before Bane got his hands on it, but I fell asleep in the midst of my work; Bane found a way to hack my security system and sneaked in quietly. Fortunately, I have this gift of feeling something or someone in danger and having a vision of the scene. So, when Bane almost got the duplicator in his hands, I suddenly woke up and caught him red-handed just in the nick of time. He was arrested and was put in jail for thirty years for being a renowned thief. Since then, I had changed the device and made a modification that only a Glaziem crest could activate it."

"Wait…" Cassidy interrupted, "why couldn't you just destroy that duplicator?"

"This is because," Mr Coronel continued patiently, "when my team invented the duplicator, they had to create a duplicating chip that could only be made out of flammable chemical, metal wire and some other precious metals that even I was not aware of. So, if we were to destroy the duplicator, it would certainly burst into flames and cause a very strong and active radiation that could spread for at least 5,000 km around the area, which would then be a great disaster! Besides, an uncontrollable riot had already broken out during that time, rendering us to run away for life; and after the riot ended, everything was destroyed in the aftermath. I didn't bother to look for the duplicator and neither did Bane as both of us thought that it had been destroyed. A few days ago, I heard the news that Bane has escaped from prison. And now that the Glaziem crest is placed on every flyer, he would have known by now that I have changed the modification, and would find a way to get all the Glaziem crests, steal the duplicator and activate it. I have to find a way to stop Bane before he gets his hands on the duplicator, for who knows what he would do with it now that he had gone through prison life."

Mr Coronel heaved a loud sigh of grief and muttered, "Why must Ridgeway Museum always put up fancy invitations with fancy bling? And out of everything on earth, why the Glaziem crest?" We could see worry in his eyes. Then, my eyes lit up. "Let US do it!" I suggested with an excited tone. "Yea!" the others shouted in agreement. Mr Coronel laughed sarcastically like we were crazy and shook his head in disapproval, "No, no, no… this is too dangerous for you. I can't let you go through with this… Moreover, you're not even completely trained yet!" and he continued laughing. "But… come on! This can be our FIRST mission! We can do it! PLEASE!!!" I pressed on. Then I gave Cassidy, Jake, Dylan and Dean the follow-what-I'm-doing look and all of us pleaded, "PLEASE!!! PLEASE!!! PRETTY PLEASE!!!"

After a few more minutes of pleading, Mr Coronel finally gave in, "Okay, but you have to follow every step I give you and you have to be very careful, as Bane is a very tricky man. We'll continue to talk about this tomorrow, okay? Your parents must be wondering why you always spend so much time in your room." All of us went into the elevator and found five seats installed, a distance away from each other, facing the elevator wall. We sat on our respective seats with our names stated on the back.

CHAPTER 13

DISCUSSION

After taking our own seats, Mr Coronel pushed a lever down and we started zooming upwards, then straight down. We were on a roller coaster ride! We could hear each other's ear-piercing screams as we went through tunnels, loops, zigzags, up and down; we went all around until it finally stopped and we were immediately back in our own rooms. When Dean and I stepped out of our seats, we were dizzy and wobbly, and could not even stand up straight. As we slumped ourselves on the carpet floor, the seats lowered into the floor, under the floor boarding and disappeared. The floor boarding was then placed back into its original position as if nothing had happened.

"Hey, you wanna watch some TV?" I asked. Dean nodded, "Sure." Both of us stepped out of our room and sat on the couch in the living room. I grabbed the remote control and switched on the television. The news channel was on, and when I was about to switch the channel, Dean stopped me. He said, "The news channel is showcasing the duplicator in Ridgeway Museum; maybe we can find some information about it." I took his point well and both of us continued watching the news and listened very carefully to every detail about it.

"Ridgeway Museum is going to showcase a newly found item in the 80's Section tomorrow night. Learning from Madison Blaine, the woman who found this item in the old countryside building in the mid-west, this item had been buried in the sand for approximately THIRTY YEARS! It is known to be a very powerful duplicator but apparently can't work anymore as it was tested out in the laboratory. This duplicator will be placed in the display case in Ridgeway Museum tomorrow night, from 7pm – 9pm, and it will be a free entry, as a normal practice for first day of opening of every newly found object, so you better hurry up!" a red head news reporter, Sally Jean, who was right in the Ridgeway Museum when she reported this segment on the television. Then, Mom walked into the living room and asked us, "Don't you kids have homework to do? And… are you watching the news? This is new… You kids usually hate the news." "Oh, ummm… actually this IS part of our homework assignment. We're supposed to watch the news and dig into it, you know, try to find more information about it. Since we just watched about Ridgeway Museum's new artifact there, can we go there tomorrow night?" I lied and Dean helped me by saying, "It's a FREE entry!" Mom agreed and we asked her if we could bring along Cassidy, Jake and Dylan with us because we were in the school project together. Mom agreed; we thanked her and ran into our room with excitement.

"That was a close one. Let's text the group about it," Dean suggested and I just plainly replied with my phone already in my hands, "One step ahead of you."

<u>UMS (chat group)</u>

Destiny :   Hello? Anybody there?

Cassidy :   Hey! Wassup!

Dean :   Did you see the news?

Cassidy :   No? Why?

Destiny :   Ridgeway Museum is displaying the duplicator tomorrow night from 7pm-9pm and it's a free entry!

Dean :   Yea! Bane might be there to steal the duplicator! We have to tell Mr Coronel before it's too late!

Jake :   Yea! But first we need to come up with a plan…

Dean :   Oh, hey Jake

Destiny :   Hi

Cassidy :   Sup bro

Jake :   Yea, hey people. Back to the plan…

Dylan :   How 'bout tomorrow night? Since it is Friday, we can all go to the museum at 7pm and stay there all the way to 9pm 'cause you'll never know when Bane might come out and steal the duplicator. Oh, don't bother to say hey; I'll take the 'heys' you gave Jake for me too.

Cassidy: Okay… But why would Bane dare to steal the duplicator tomorrow night since there would be many people there? I mean, hello! Free entry! No one would miss an opportunity like that.

Dean: That's the point! Bane would steal the duplicator then because Ridgeway Museum will be so crowded that it'll take some time to notice if the duplicator is missing.

Cassidy: Oh… I get it… But we should discuss this with Mr Coronel first before we take matters into our own hands.

Destiny: You're right, but we'll meet up with Mr Coronel tomorrow 'cause we still have school and I bet all of us have a ton of homework to do.

Jake: Yea… you're right. Well, off to the books!

Cassidy: Yep. Bye.

Dylan: Bye

Destiny: See ya!

Dean: I am now offline…

Chapter 14

SCIENCE MAYHEM

The next morning, just like the previous day, Cassidy, Jake, Dylan, Dean and I walked to school. During Science lesson, Ms. Voila was teaching us how to dissect a frog. She warned us to only squeeze all the frog's insides out in the sink. Ms. Voila chose a partner for everybody – Cassidy and me, Jake and Dean, but poor Dylan had to partner Angie from The Goth and Alex and Aida partnered each other. Cassidy, Jake, Dean and I felt sorry for Dylan so we asked if Dylan could join Jake and Dean's group and after a few minutes of pleading from The Goth and us, Ms. Voila finally gave in. So Cassidy and I partnered each other and Jake, Dean and Dylan were a group, so as The Goth. Everyone else had a partner.

Once everyone was given a frog in a tray, we lined up to squeeze the frog's insides out in the sink. As we were lining up, The Goth who were behind Cassidy and me, stepped out of the line and tried to cut in front of Cassidy and me. Before they could cut the line, I stepped forward and said,

"No cuts. Everybody's lining up." Cassidy nudged me and gave me a what-do-you-think-you're-doing look and I just gave her an everything-is-gonna-be-fine look back, and as I turned to give her that look, I could see Jake, Dean and Dylan's anxious and worry looks.

Then, Aida said, "Oh, so you have a backbone eh? Let's see what I can do about that." She had a dark look on her face, and then turned to Alex and snapped her finger. Alex held up the frog in her hand and squeezed it at my face. But being smart, I turned my head sideward just in time to miss the insides of the frog hitting my face. Then, Aida had a bit of annoyance in her face and she shouted, "Angie!" Apparently Angie knew exactly what Aida wanted her to do; she grabbed the frog from Alex's hand and squirted the frog's insides on my brand new white shirt. I didn't have enough time to avoid that so gooey blobs of the frog's insides splattered at the side of shirt. I gasped then thought to myself: I can't give her the satisfaction. So, to do that, I will 'unsatisfy' her by being satisfied! It worked in my old school; let's see if it works here. So be POSITIVE!

I smiled at The Goth and thanked them, "Thank you! This is a brand new shirt and I was ALSO thinking that it needed colour! Now that there's a mixture of them, I can paint a design on it during art class later on! You have given me inspiration, Angie! Oh, Aida, how your leadership has inspired me! And Alex, so close, yet so far. Good luck with your improvements!" I smirked and waved then headed to the girl's bathroom to wash off the blobs on my shirt. The Goth stood there in confusion; their minds went blank, as they still could not believe my reaction towards them. Before they could think of cutting in front of Cassidy, Cassidy said, "Didn't you hear? At the back of the line!" I was glad my confidence has made Cassidy bolder in front of The Goth.

After washing off the blobs on my shirt in the girl's bathroom, there was still a stain on my shirt but I knew that a little bit of painting over it would make it better and actually nicer. To be honest, after saying what I said to The Goth, it wasn't as fake as I thought it would be.

When I got back into the class, everybody had already squeezed all the frog's insides out in the sink and Cassidy was waiting for me. When I sat down on my seat, everybody started clapping and cheering for me. I was caught in the moment, and then Cassidy pulled me to her and said, "Destiny! You're the only one who has ever stood up to The Goth so far and everyone looks up to you now! I can't believe you are so AWESOME! Girl, you've got a whole new reputation here; you're going to be popular! But, The Goth might still want to get back at you for that, so be careful!" "Thanks! This is just something I learned in my old school: if someone wants to 'unsatisfy' you, 'unsatisfy' him or her by being satisfied! So just be POSITIVE!" I replied.

During art class, I used blue and pink fabric paint to paint a Hawaiian flower on the side of my shirt where I got the stain. After painting the flower and adding a few more small details to it, the stain was totally covered and my plain white shirt was completely renewed! When I put down my paintbrush, the renewed shirt immediately drew in a lot of attention! The Goth just stared and ignored the creative design on my stained shirt. I purposely went up to them and thanked them once again for squeezing the frog's insides on my shirt so that I could make my plain white shirt look nicer. As expected, they just scowled at me and looked away in disgust.

CHAPTER 15

THE PLAN

After school, while Cassidy, Jake, Dylan, Dean and I were walking home, Jake praised me, "Destiny! You were awesome when you stood up to The Goth!" "Thanks," I replied, blushing a little. Then Dean said, "Destiny always stood up to the bullies in our old school. Whenever the bully had something to say, Destiny would always have something in mind to talk back. Talking back is just in her blood." "It's true..." I agreed then giggled a little.

When we got home, all of us went directly to our own homes then met in the elevator. As we were in the elevator and jumping on the trampoline, we discussed over our plan and decided to tell Mr Coronel. When the elevator door slid open, all of us ran out to Mr Coronel and took turns explaining our plan to him. Our plan was...

First, we would go to Ridgeway Museum for a look out, especially at the duplicator display case. Then, we would stay there all the way until the museum closed. We could speak to each other through the earpiece and with the new cap cam (a new invention Mr Coronel created - a camera hidden in a cap), which Cassidy would be wearing. Mr Coronel would be able to see our surroundings. When Mr Coronel spotted Bane, he would inform us. Then, all of us would protect the duplicator in its display case and not let Bane come near it.

After some thoughts, Mr Coronel responded, "That seems like a simple enough plan but I think that'll be too simple. Bane is a mastermind of things and being an infamous criminal himself, he would have more accomplices with him. If I let you all do this, you have to promise me to be very careful... and I'll support you with all the necessary gadgets you'll need for your mission."

Cassidy, Jake, Dylan, Dean and I squealed in delight and celebrated, "Yay! Our first mission!" Then, we saw Mom calling for Dean and me on the screen. "Dean! Destiny! It's almost 6pm! You better eat your dinner before you leave for the museum! I can heat up the leftover lasagna for you guys if you want!" Mr Coronel then pulled out a radio system and gestured Dean and me to come to him, and then said, "Press this button and say what you need to say into this device, the sound will transmit through another device installed in your room."

I pressed the button and said, "It's okay, Mom! We'll eat over there!" "Yea! We still have to pack our things to bring for later!" Dean continued. Then, we could see Mom listening from outside the door and she replied back, "Okay!"

Mr Coronel hurried us into the gadget room and said, "We better hurry, as you all have not much time. He gestured us to sit on the sack bags on the floor, then pressed a few buttons on the desk of the gadget room. Suddenly, the floor in front of us flipped over, and five different gadgets laid there. Mr Coronel explained what the gadgets were meant for. The gadgets were a pod that emits smoke when impacted on ground, a laser pen to be used only in an emergency, a small bottle of spray can that contains some chemicals to make someone fall asleep, a Swiss army knife and an extension cord belt.

Each of us was given all five items and we set off to the Ridgeway Museum. When we got there, the museum owner, Mr Flake started the opening by giving an introduction about the duplicator and expressing gratitude to those who had helped fund the showcase of the duplicator, followed by the ribbon cutting ceremony. Immediately after the event, Cassidy, Jake, Dylan, Dean and I rushed into the hall together with the crowd. Since it was too crowded, we held hands to form a human chain so as not to separate from one another. We squeezed our way to the front, and finally got to the front of the display showcase of the duplicator. As all of us surrounded the duplicator, we examined the people around us, observing if there was anyone suspicious lurking around, mostly if Bane was around.

After waiting for an hour of sitting beside the duplicator's display showcase and talking about when Bane was going to show up, we started to get hungry. Coincidentally, Mr Flake announced, "We are going to take a break now and we are now serving a buffet of tea and snacks down the hall. You all may follow me into the hall now." and headed into the hall while the crowd followed behind him. Jake stood up and started following the crowd when Cassidy quickly stopped him and asked, "What do you think you're doing?" "Getting a snack?" Jake replied with oblivion written all over his face. Then I explained, "You can't possibly leave? I mean… Bane hasn't even shown up yet… and now could be his chance to steal the duplicator while everybody's eating in the hall." "That's true you know," Dylan continued. Then Dean, while standing up, backed up Jake and said, "I think that it's fine. Jake and I can go get some snacks for all of us and you guys can stay here and look out for Bane. We'll be back in no time." Cassidy, Dylan and I finally agreed and Jake and Dean went to the hall to get the snacks.

As Cassidy, Dylan and I continued observing our surroundings for Bane, I realised that we were the only ones here and everyone else was in the hall, stuffing themselves with the buffet of pastries and snacks. Shortly after, Jake and Dean were walking towards us with plates of snacks and pastries. I suddenly spotted a suspicious man wearing dark sunglasses and an overcoat hoodie approaching the display showcase. I nudged Cassidy and Dylan who were both sitting beside me almost falling asleep and informed them about the suspicious man. They looked in the direction of the suspicious man, and I spoke into the earpiece, which everyone was using to listen to whatever was transmitted, and asked Mr Coronel, who was at the other line, if the man was Bane. Mr Coronel answered back, "Could be… but you should investigate first… 'Cos we can't be too sure and we can't be too safe." I agreed and replied, "Ok. Jake, Dylan, Dean, round the duplicator and Cassidy and I will improvise and distract the suspicious man. We will try to see his face or at least get his face shown in Cassidy's cap cam."

CHAPTER 16

THE MISSION

Jake and Dean hurried over with the plate of snacks in their hands and stood around the duplicator with Dylan pretending to admire it. The suspicious man was hesitantly walking towards the duplicator, and then Cassidy and I popped up in front of him. He was taken aback then tried to make his way through us. I started improvising, "Hi! Ummm… We… we are looking for the girl's toilet. Do you know where it is?" As I was saying that, Cassidy tried to bend down a little, hoping to catch a glimpse of the man's face in the cap cam as he was looking down, but to no avail. The man just shook his head and tried to walk away. Cassidy quickly extended her leg and the man tripped over it; his hoodie flew from his head and he bumped his head on the floor. I smacked my palm on my forehead and gave Cassidy a did-you-seriously-have-to-do-that look but Cassidy just gave me an oops-ha-ha-sorry-too-late-already look. She quickly apologised profusely and helped the man up. As the man was no longer wearing a hoodie, we could see his face. He was a balding man with freckles and pimples all over his face. Jake quickly asked Mr Coronel through the earpiece devise if that was Bane. Mr Coronel just sighed and said, "No… You just injured a "guinea pig"… His name is Revlon Kazowski, a new "guinea pig" in a lab to test out medication for approval for human consumption but apparently there were unknown side effects, which were pimples and freckles… The doctors are still finding a cure for this…"

As Mr Coronel explained this, Revlon realised that he was no longer wearing his hoodie and ran away screaming and covering his face. Cassidy and I walked towards the boys with disappointed looks. I sighed and said, "Not only did we injure a poor innocent man, but we also did not find Bane." "It's going to be okay, Bane would appear soon," Jake said and gave me an encouraging smile. "Well, at least we know why he was wearing a hoodie." Dean said and laughed a little, trying to ease the tension. "Freeze!" Mr Coronel shouted through the other line of the earpiece. All of us froze in shock and Mr Coronel said, "Cassidy, turn a little back to your right." And Cassidy did accordingly. "Look," Mr Coronel continued, "do you see the man in the employee uniform heading your way?" "Ya?" the five of us replied together. "That's Bane." Mr Coronel confirmed with a strong and firm tone.

Bane walked closer to us then, with a warm and gentle tone, said, "Hi, I'm Blaine Baxter, the inventory staff here. Would you all please move away from the display case? I need to remove the duplicator from its place for the examiner to take a further examination as a dangerous trigger was found to set on it." Before Bane could take it away, Mr Coronel informed us through the earpiece not to let Bane take it. Dean therefore reacted quickly, "Why? I thought before anything is placed in the museum, there would be months of observation and examination to verify that the item is safe. And only when it is confirmed safe, it can then be placed in the museum." "Yea! Everybody knows that. You're an employee staff, so you should know that, right?" I backed up Dean. Bane just stood there and started stammering and thinking of what to say then. He finally replied, "That's true, but we can't be too sure, right? So if you would please, move away." By then, Bane was growing more agitated and trying to quickly get the duplicator and make a run for it. "Actually we CAN be too sure, the highest authority of examination always confirm the safety of an object through many papers before it is allowed to be displayed in a museum." Dean blabbed on about museums and authorities that made all of us confused, even Bane. Then, Bane interrupted and with an annoyed tone, he said, "Well then you give me no choice!" Bane shoved us away from the duplicator's display case and I quickly dug out the first thing I grabbed - the small bottle of spray can, or as the five of us call it, the sleepy spray. Then I shouted, "Well, desperate times come for desperate measures" and sprayed sleepy gas at Bane's face. Bane was caught off guard and fell on the floor and into sleep.

All of us started giving each other high-5s for our success. Then, Mr Coronel congratulated us and instructed, "Okay, now that you have got Bane into a trance, it will take a while before he wakes up. So, bring him back to the lab first and see what we can get out of him." "How? It would be weird for everyone to see us carrying a sleeping man out of the museum…" Cassidy asked Mr Coronel. Mr Coronel thought for a while and suggested us to use the extension cord belt and exit through the window at the ceiling and out onto the roof and a helicopter would come for us. We were all in shock upon hearing the word "helicopter" from Mr Coronel. "A helicopter? You're going to land a helicopter on the roof? Don't you think people might notice a helicopter on the roof?" Jake asked astonishingly. "Yes, a helicopter. Anyways, the people would be too busy stuffing their faces with food to even notice. Now go!" "How do you work this thing?" I asked. "Just pull the belt clipping," Dylan replied. I pulled my belt clipping and aimed at the ceiling. It shot right next to the roof window. I tugged on the string, which connected the belt clipping and me, and the next thing I knew was that I flew across the room landing right next to the roof window. I was amazed and gave them a thumbs-up as I looked down at them. I climbed out of the window and onto the roof. Then Cassidy was next; she did the same thing as I did but lost balance as she landed next to the roof window. I quickly held her hand and pulled her out onto the roof. She thanked me for saving her life and her heartbeat was racing as she did so. Dylan was next, followed by Jake and Dean who were carrying Bane as they shot up to the ceiling. Jake and Dean landed on the ceiling next to the window. Dylan, Cassidy and I helped Bane out onto the roof and Jake and Dean climbed out after him.

CHAPTER 17

TO THE LAB

After a few minutes, the helicopter arrived and landed on the roof of the museum. Mr Coronel stepped out of the helicopter to help Bane in, then followed by Dylan, Cassidy, Jake, Dean and me. Mr Coronel sat at the front seat with the pilot. "This is SO COOL!" Cassidy exclaimed as she took her seat. "Yea! This is my first time riding a helicopter." I shouted back. "It's a first for all of us." Jake continued. Then I asked, "Really? I thought you all have been in the UMS longer than we have so you all would have been doing this for a long time." "Nah, we've only been training. We had to wait for a few more members, which were you guys, before we could actually go for a mission." Dylan explained.

Then as the pilot turned on the engine, suddenly, the helicopter jerked. The pilot looked back and shouted, "Oh no! We're being attacked by that jet!" Mr Coronel turned back and shouted, "It must be Bane's accomplices coming for Bane! Pilot! We have to go faster!" The pilot nodded his head, started increasing the speed and took off. Then,

Bane's accomplices started shooting us with guns and the helicopter was hit so off balance that I, who was sitting at the side of the helicopter, was thrown out. I quickly grabbed onto the hand railings and started screaming. Dean hurriedly grabbed my arm but the wind was strong enough to almost blow me away. At that moment, Jake extended his hand and grabbed my other arm. Without thinking, Jake and Dean told me to let go of the railing. "Are you crazy? I could fall!!!" I raised my voice in desperation. "Just trust us!" Jake and Dean shouted together.

I hesitantly let go of the railings and Jake and Dean pulled me in. When I got back onto my seat, the pilot quickly pressed a button on the emergency panel and the doors of the helicopter slid down to secure the helicopter. My heart was palpitating wildly and my face was as white as a sheet of paper; I was still in shock and petrified. At that moment, the first time ever, I hugged Dean and he didn't resist and hugged me back tightly. I was almost tearing up after the trauma I just went through and was speechless. I just faintly said, "thanks…" Dean then replied, "No prob. I won't let you get hurt…" and I gave him a weak smile. Soon Bane's accomplices lost track of us and we were back into the lab.

When we got into the lab, some of Mr Coronel's workers carried Bane's sleeping body into a transparent capsule. Mr Coronel warned us that Bane's accomplices would be wandering around, trying to get Bane back, so all of us have to be very careful. "You mean 'big people' are out there trying to get us 'small people'?" Cassidy asked with a quaky voice. "Well, what a great impression to our first few days in this neighbourhood…" Dean said sarcastically. After Mr Coronel gave us an extra warning, we went into the elevator and pressed a new button, which Mr Coronel had installed. It was the 'TREE' button; it would transport us to the big elm tree in the field. Then, we went back to our own separate homes, hoping that the next day would be better.

CHAPTER 18

CONFESSIONS

The next morning (a Saturday, which means no school), when Dean and I were taking our own sweet time eating breakfast, our phones (which were right beside us on the dining table) beeped. We looked at them and found that Cassidy notified everybody to meet up in the elevator to the lab now. Dean and I sneaked past Mom who was busy washing dishes and Dad who was busy reading newspapers, and ran into our room. We, as usual, flipped open the light switch panel, scanned our thumbprints and landed in the elevator. Cassidy, Jake and Dylan were already bouncing on the trampoline elevator waiting for us to arrive.

Cassidy spoke up, "Okay, good, they're here. Now, what is it you wanted to tell us?" Dylan calmly said, "Bane has woken up." Cassidy, Jake, Dean and I gasped quietly and Dean queried, "So what happened?" "I don't know yet... Dad said... ummm, I mean Mr Coronel said that he would explain to us when we get to the lab."

Soon, the elevator reached the lab and all of us hurriedly jumped out and ran to Mr Coronel who apparently was expecting us to jump out as he was standing a distance away from the elevator. All five of us ran to him and started bursting numerous questions in his face, such as, "What happened?" "Did Bane say anything?" "Where is he?" "What are you going to do about him?" and so on and so forth. Mr Coronel waved his hand in our faces gesturing us to stop our persistent questions. After our noise died down, he led us into the room where Bane was still held captive in the capsule.

When Bane saw us, he grew purple with rage and was fuming mad. He started shouting, "You RASCALS! Getting in the way! I almost got it! But YOU!" Bane stared at Mr Coronel, "YOU ALWAYS GET IN THE WAY OF EVERYTHING I DO! If it weren't because of you, I would have been the world's renowned scientist! But YOU had to get ALL the credits for everything I DID!" Mr Coronel stepped forward and pressed a button on Bane's capsule; Bane's mouth kept moving but we couldn't hear a word. "Am I deaf?" Jake said and started shaking his head vigorously. Mr Coronel held his head firm and said, "No. I muted the sound so whatever he says, we cannot hear, and no matter how loud he gets, nothing can pass through the sound barrier of the capsule. He may just shout until his head bursts."

"Is this why you called us here? To see his head burst?" Dean asked looking puzzled. "No," Mr Coronel continued, "We are going to put Bane back in prison, but first we need to run a few tests to find out why he is so mad and why he wants the duplicator so badly…" "Isn't it obvious?" I asked, "I mean, you don't need to run tests on someone you've known almost your whole life. Bane is mad at you because you've got all the credits. Is it really true that Bane was actually the one who invented the things but you had received all the credits? Don't you think that he wants the duplicator back so that he can take back what rightfully belongs to him? Don't you see that he only wants to be recognised for his inventions? Think, Mr Coronel, has he ever had any credit at all? Have you ever given him some credit at all?"

Mr Coronel went into deep thought and finally said solemnly, "you're right, Destiny… I did get all the credits and now that I think about it… I didn't give him any but he never gave my ideas a chance. When I had ideas, he just threw them into the bin; he never listened to me. I knew he was better than me but I wanted to prove that I was smart too. So I took the credit for what he did. And… and…" Mr Coronel turned to Bane, pressed the un-mute button on the capsule and continued, "I'm sorry… I… I just wanted you to listen to me. My self-esteem got the better of me… I'm sorry, Bane… I really am." Bane looked at Mr Coronel's eyes and then confessed, "I'm sorry too… I should've listened to you… but I got greedy… I'm sorry."

While all of us were touched by what we heard and saw, Cassidy suddenly freaked out, "well, not to rain on your parade here but what are we supposed to do NOW? Does Bane go back to prison or WHAT??? How about Bane's accomplices? Are they still out there to get us?" "Well, why don't we both turn ourselves in? If you don't go back to prison, the police will definitely track you down and you'll get into an even worse trouble. I however can't let you go in alone either, for the hurt I've done to you…" Mr Coronel suggested to Bane with a warm smile. "WHAT!?! Are you CRAZY? What about the UMS? What about EVERYTHING? What are WE gonna do when you go?" Cassidy started shouting and freaking out. I told Jake to hold his arms out behind Cassidy and Cassidy was like stammering, "what… what are… what…?" I grabbed the sleepy spray out of my bag and sprayed it at her face. She fell fast asleep and into the arms of Jake. "Nice catch!" Dean gave Jake a thumbs-up and I just smiled. "Well, we'll leave now and let you two sort out whatever it is you need to sort out. Oh, and by the way, is there something that can make Cassidy wake up faster? Maybe a walk in the park can make ourselves clear our minds." I asked. Mr Coronel replied, "Just turn the sleepy spray's lid at the direction the arrow says 'Awake' on the cover and spray her, and she'll be up after a couple of minutes." As the boys dragged Cassidy into the elevator, I sprayed Cassidy's face with the reverse effect of the sleepy spray. As we waited for Cassidy to wake up, we laid Cassidy in the middle of the trampoline; then Jake, Dylan, Dean and I started jumping up and down on the trampoline and watched Cassidy's body bounce up and down. Soon, Cassidy woke up.

Chapter 19

KIDNAPPED

After being transported to the big elm tree, Cassidy and I sat on the swings while Jake, Dylan and Dean sat on the grass in front of us. We were discussing on what would happen if Mr Coronel and Bane went to jail, with our minds filled with questions hoping to find answers: What would become of us? Would the UMS shut down? Are we going to break up? What would happen? At that moment, we heard the bushes behind us rattling but we were busy enough to ignore it.

Mom called for Dean and me to buy some groceries for her in a convenience store a few blocks away from the neighbourhood. She gave us a list and some money; she also told us that we could buy sweets if there was any small change left. The five of us then set off and headed towards the convenience store.

As we were about to open the door to the convenience store, a black piece of cloth was put over my eyes. Apparently I was blindfolded, and so were the others. I had no clue on what was happening and I couldn't see if Cassidy, Jake,

Dylan and Dean were alright but I knew they were still somewhere with me as I heard their cries and screams and I, too, was screaming for help. But apparently no one was there to help us. I felt somebody tying my hands together and carrying me away, I let out an ear-piercing scream and the person who was carrying me, whispered in my ear with a deep and menacing tone, "Shut up! Or you're not going to have a tomorrow!" I was so scared that I just let out a short high-pitch "eep" sound then quickly shut my mouth. As all of us were being carried away, we were all trying to struggle free but to no avail.

We were thrown in the back of a vehicle and were driven away. It was hot and stuffy in there; beads of perspiration trickled down my cheek, and as I sat there, thoughts of horror scenes and terrifying images went through my mind. My heart was beating wildly. I just couldn't imagine what horrible things would happen to us. Soon, the vehicle screeched to a halt and we were carried out.

After a while, our blindfolds were whipped off. Cassidy, Jake, Dylan, Dean and I found ourselves sitting on wooden chairs, a distance away from one another. Jake sat at the most right side, then me, Dean, Cassidy and Dylan. We were in a room with concrete walls and floor tiles, and there were only two windows and a door across the room. Three muscular men stood in front of us. Their arms were heavily tattooed and had scars on their faces, they seemed like body-builders. I thought to myself: 'they must be Bane's accomplices and they're trying to get Bane back. They must know that we're involved in taking Bane away... what should we do now? What CAN we do now? Most importantly, what are THEY gonna do to US?'

As I sat there freaking in my mind, the man standing in the middle spoke up in a deep voice, "Where's Bane?" "Who?" Dean asked back, trying to struggle free from the rope tied around his hands behind the chair (all our hands were tied behind the chair we were sitting on, making it impossible for us to struggle free). "Don't act dumb and by the way, those ropes will get tighter as long as you try to struggle free. And we know you know where he is. So speak up, or else…" the man replied with anger in his eyes. "Or else WHAT?" Dean shouted with daring eyes. This time, Cassidy, Jake, Dylan and I stared at him and gave him the what-on-earth-do-you-think-you're-doing-are-you trying-to-get-us-killed look.

The man gave us an evil grin, which made all five of us petrified except Dean who was trying to act a little bit braver but we could still see that he was scared. The man took the wooden chair beside him and with a loud shout; with all his strength he forcefully threw the chair on the floor. There was a loud bang and after opening our eyes, we saw the once properly stable chair broke apart and even a small crack appeared on the grey cement floor. All of us stared wide-eyed at the broken chair and our mouths went dry, our hearts were racing and our throats were tightening. "So? SPEAK UP!" the man standing at the right shouted impatiently. "Relax Garial," the middleman said, "They'll eventually crack."

Chapter 20

THE ESCAPE

Just then, there was a loud bang at the door. The three men walked towards the door and started talking inaudibly to someone at the doorstep. Then, Garial turned back and shouted at us, "DON'T MOVE!" Soon after, the three of them headed out and slammed the door behind them.

"WHAT ARE WE GOING TO DO???" Cassidy shouted in a whispered panicky tone. "Hey! I think I can reach my Swiss army knife!" Jake exclaimed in a hushed voice. He quietly pulled out his Swiss army knife from his back pocket, and cut the ropes off his hands. After a few seconds, Jake cut free from the ropes. He dashed to my side, as I was right beside him. After cutting off the ropes free for me, he went to Dean. I whipped out my Swiss army knife from my hoodie shirt pocket (luckily they didn't inspect our pockets or anything), and ran to cut Cassidy's rope loose then Dylan's.

While still recovering from the rope burns (which made our wrists really sore), I whispered to the group, "So, what are we gonna do now? The three men can come back in the room anytime!" "We can escape through the back window." Dylan whispered back. There were only two windows in the room, one next to the door and the other one opposite it. All of us agreed to climb out of the back window opposite to the door. Apparently we didn't wait for the right timing as when Jake (who was the last person to climb out) was climbing out of the window, Garial turned his head and looked through the window next to the door and saw Jake climbing out. He shouted at the top of his lungs, "THEY'RE ESCAPING!!!" Once all of us heard that, we quickly ran away. Although we didn't know where we were, we just kept on running.

But not for long, the three men caught up with us. As they were almost about to grab us, Cassidy let out an ear-piercing scream. We could see that she was terrified as cold sweat trickled down her forehead. She quickly pulled out the Taser pen she clipped onto her shorts, and without thinking at all, she tased the man nearest to him. The man had a shock and fell onto the floor. "Nice job, Cassidy!" I praised her. Taking out my Taser pen, I shocked Garial followed by the middleman. Then, Dean also took out his Taser pen and tased the three men again and said, "You can never be too sure." "It will take at least an hour before they regain consciousness." Dylan responded. After all that, Cassidy, Jake, Dylan, Dean and I had a group hug congratulating one another. Then, I talked through the earpiece informing Mr Coronel that we didn't know where we were and needed help. As the five of us waited for his response, I thought to myself, "Is he going to answer? What if he doesn't? What's going to happen?" Soon, Mr Coronel responded, "Are all of you okay? I can track you down through your earpiece; I designed it with a GPS tracker so I can find you wherever you are. Are you at a concrete warehouse?" "Yea," the five of us responded together. "Okay, I'm on my way." Mr Coronel replied.

Soon, we heard a loud noise from the sky and saw a jet! It landed a few meters in front of us and out came Mr Coronel and Bane. Mr Coronel ran to us and checked if we were okay, then all of us got into the jet. A few men came out from the jet and carried the three men on the floor into the jet and stored them in the same capsule as Bane's. Soon, the jet took off and then I nervously asked Mr Coronel, "So are you two going to jail?" Mr Coronel and Bane let out a deep laugh, and Mr Coronel replied, "Well, of course not! All of you have passed the test!" "What?" Cassidy puzzled. "Well, this whole mission was to test your abilities and to see if all of you can work together and now you've all passed! There was never any real harm. Bane is not my enemy partner; he is my brother! The three men were robots and they weren't going to harm you. We were planning this the whole time since Dean and Destiny got here and all your parents are aware of this. In fact, all of your parents were part of UMS before, but now they are retired, so they would like to pass their roles to the next generation, which is all of you! Of course we didn't tell Cassidy, Jake and Dylan about this as it was supposed to test what you would actually do when you encounter these situations during your missions. And I am glad to say that you all have passed!" Turning to Dean and me, Mr Coronel continued, "But, it is Dean and Destiny's decision if they want to stay or leave." "Okay, first of all, we went through all of this just for a test!?! We were tied up, blindfolded, and Destiny almost flew out of the helicopter and now you're asking us if we want to stay!?!" Dean shouted, then turning to me. We looked at each other, smirked and nodded our heads at each other, then exclaimed together, "OF COURSE WE'RE STAYING!!!" Mr Coronel, Bane, Cassidy, Jake and Dylan looked a little scared at first then started laughing. All of us laughed together, marking the new beginning for the whole team of us.

CHAPTER 21

NEW BEGINNINGS

After all the drama and laughter, we headed back to the lab only to find our families waiting for us to arrive and to celebrate our success. Mr Coronel gave Cassidy, Jake, Dylan, Dean and me promotional badges and we were stated the "Official UMS Spies". After getting our badges, we had a huge party ceremony with all the other UMS members and spies. The lab was decorated with streamers and balloons, and a huge banner was plastered on the wall which written "CONGRATULATIONS!!!" We had a scrumptious and mouth-watering buffet, mingling with the other UMS spies and playing numerous games.

As the party was about to end, a loud alarm bell went off. Everybody was startled. "Oh no!" Mr Coronel gasped under his breath, went to his desk, pressed a few buttons and a huge screen came down from the wall with a map shown on it, and a blinking red dot caught our attention. Mr Coronel clicked on the blinking red dot and it showed footage of people heading into a mall and running out crazily, screams and cries were heard. Mr Coronel then said to Cassidy, Jake, Dylan, Dean and me, "Well, today's your lucky day! Your first official mission! Good luck!" Everybody started clapping and the five of us bid everybody farewell and headed directly into the jet that was waiting for us at the station.

As we sat in the jet, my heart was beating fast with anticipation and excitement. I never knew that moving to this place could change our lives forever...

ABOUT THE AUTHOR

Priscilla Way Yun was a 12-year-old student with the Nan Hua Primary School in Singapore. Under the encouragement of her parents, she started this 'little project' by writing up this storybook immediately after her important Primary School Leaving Examination (PSLE) in October 2013, to mark a milestone in her life. The objective of the publication is to make monetary provision to the poor and needy families possible, responding to a burden planted in the parents' hearts after an impactful trip in June 2013.

Printed in the United States
By Bookmasters